SASHA visits KUALA LUMPUR

Illustrated by Alpana Ahuja
Written by Shamini Flint

Enjoy!
Shamini
2010

Book Two: Sasha in Asia

Sasha is visiting Kuala Lumpur.

Kuala Lumpur is the capital city of Malaysia.

Sasha sees a beautiful old building on the other side of a river.

"Mamma, what's that?"

"It is a mosque called Masjid Jamek, Sasha."

Masjid Jamek was built at the meeting point of the two rivers that run through Kuala Lumpur.

Alpana

"Mamma, look how tall those buildings are!"

The Twin Towers are among the tallest buildings in the world.

Sasha puts her hands in the air.

"Mamma, am I as tall as the Twin Towers?"

Mamma laughs.

Alpana

Sasha and Mamma stop for lunch.

Their table is on a pavement outside the restaurant.

Sasha watches people go by as she tucks into her delicious fried rice.

A cat waits under the table for scraps!

Alpana

Sasha and Mamma pass a rubber plantation on the outskirts of Kuala Lumpur.

There are rows and rows of rubber trees.

Sasha stops to watch a man tapping rubber.

The milky white sap of the rubber tree drips into a cup.

"What do they do with the rubber, Mamma?"

"Rubber is used to make many things like car tyres and balloons, Sasha."

Alpena

That night Mamma takes Sasha on a very special boat trip.

"Mamma, what are all those lights?"

"They are fireflies, Sasha!"

The fireflies look like tiny stars twinkling on the banks of the river.

The next morning Sasha visits a park called the Lake Gardens.

Sasha is very excited because Mamma lets her feed the deer.

Mamma admires the beautiful orchids and the view of the lake.

Alpona

Sasha is thirsty.

"Mamma, may we stop for a drink?"

Mamma buys Sasha a coconut at a fruit stall.

Sasha drinks the juice of the coconut with a straw.

"Mamma, it's delicious!"

Sasha tastes spiky durians, purple mangosteens and hairy rambutans.

Can you spot the fruits that Sasha tastes?

Alpana

Sasha is on a jungle walkway built high in the trees.

Two magpie robins and a bulbul stop to say "hello".

Can you spot them?

Maybe they think Sasha is a bird too!

That evening, Mamma takes Sasha to the Bangsar *pasar malam*.

Pasar malam means 'night market' in Malay.

There are many colourful stalls selling everything from fish to flowers.

What else is being sold at the Bangsar *pasar malam*?

Alpana

The next day it is time to go home.

"May we come again soon, Mamma?"

"Certainly, Sasha!"

Mamma and Sasha catch a train at the Kuala Lumpur train station and set off for home.

KUALA LUMPUR
Alpana

Sasha visits
the Botanic Gardens

Sasha visits the Zoo

Sasha goes Shopping

Sasha visits Sentosa Island

Sasha visits the Bird Park

Sasha visits the Museums

Sasha visits Bali

Sasha visits
Kuala Lumpur

Sasha visits Hong Kong
(Available in Mandarin)

Sasha visits Bangkok

Sasha visits Singapore
(Available in Mandarin)

Sasha visits Beijing
(Available in Mandarin)

Sasha visits Tokyo

Sasha visits Mumbai